The Messy Pirates

Nicole Caruso LaBrocca

Illustrated by Lizy J Campbell

Messy Pirates Book 1: By **Nicole Caruso LaBrocca**

Copyright © 2021. All rights reserved.

Published by Pen It! Publications, LLC in the U.S.A. 812-371-4128
www.penitpublications.com

ISBN: 978-1-63984-119-6

Illustrated by Lizy J Campbell

This Book Belongs To

_____

On a bustling boat in the rolling sea,

with the figurehead of a wailing banshee,

Smoothly sailed kindly pirate Captain Selene,

whose massive ship was never clean.

Stashing their treasure everywhere,

Selene's bubbly crew did not care.

The cheerful crew would sing, dance and play,

continuing fun all through the day.

And though being a pirate was quite a new gig,

dear Captain Selene joined with a song and a jig.

But the new captain really did not have a clue,

as to what a normal pirate simply must do.

Having heisted successfully the previous night,

their booty pile was quite a sight.

Lifting treasures from the mean and the greedy,

Selene gives quite much to the hardworking and needy.

The rest of the loot was shared equally with her crew,

because with her gang, she was honorable and true.

Captain Selene's crew sang aloud,

while some gloated with looks so proud.

Basking in happiness with drinks and laughter,

clueless and thoughtless of what could come after.

Then like a beacon of towering light,

Selene's ship caught the eye of old Captain Might.

When he saw the treasure of sparkling jewels,

he said to his crew, "Oh what meandering fools!"

Because the code that every pirate must heed,

is that cleaning, is the most important deed.

Spic and span were pirate ships in the day,

reminded old Captain Might before any fray.

Upon the order from old Captain Might,

his big brave crew stood ready to fight.

Stumbling over the shimmering stones,

Selene's silly crew settled in their zones.

But since their treasure pile rose so tall,

they couldn't find a single cannonball.

"Fire the cannons! It's time to shoot!"

and Captain Selene yelled, "Hurry, save our loot!"

But Selene's crew was singing a battle song,

and so they heard the poor Captain wrong.

With a raise of a brow and the shrug of their shoulders,

the crew followed their orders like obedient soldiers.

20

And in another bad and unwise blunder,

they chose to shoot out all of their plunder.

Selene gasped in utter despair,

as the gold and jewels flew through the air.

With his hull intact and his heavy boat filled,

Old Captain Might and his crew were more than thrilled.

The jewels and the gold were easily hidden,

in clean boxes and shelves where clutter was forbidden.

Then old Captain Might sailed away in delight,

after having won such an easy peasy fight.

And knowing that he would always defeat,

many a pirate who refused to be neat.

After seeing her gold float briskly away,

Selene said, "Messy is surely not the way!"

She quietly made the simple admission,

that being tidy was a necessary condition.

Now Selene's boat is spotlessly clean,

and not a single speck of dust can be seen.

And when the challenges start to get rough,

her shipshape crew always stands tough.

From a sturdy bow to a bowing stern,

a clean ship is what Captain Selene holds firm.

Yes, clean is the order of the day,

and it's clear that Selene will get her way.

The End!

Nicole Caruso LaBrocca is a passionate Author who spends her free time writing away in New Jersey. Hailing from the same area, her unquenchable passion for all things creative began early on and it has stayed with her ever since. What started as epic reveries, turned into ideas that soon transformed into stories.

When she isn't spilling her soul on paper, Nicole enjoys the simple things in life, such as playing soccer, reading, kayaking, and a little one-on-one time with Mother Nature. And in case anyone was wondering... Nicole holds a B.S. in Computer Science & Information Systems. Nicole Caruso LaBrocca is the Author of *The Messy Pirates* series, *Vita-Men: The Heroes Inside Us (Attack of the Sugar Goblins)*, and *Eat Your Vegetables!* and encourages you to watch for more books coming soon.

64067291R00022